DILLY

AND T...

'Land ho, and s... ...imbers!' shouted Dilly. He ...as waving a stick with some old rope tied to it. 'Your punishment be one thousand lashes, ooh aargh!'

TONY BRADMAN

DiLLY

AND THE PIRATES

Illustrated by Susan Hellard

MAMMOTH

First published in Great Britain 1992
by Piccadilly Press Ltd
Published 1994 by Mammoth
an imprint of Reed Consumer Books Ltd
Michelin House, 81 Fulham Road, London SW3 6RB
and Auckland, Melbourne, Singapore and Toronto

Reprinted 1994

ISBN 0 7497 1654 1

A CIP catalogue record for this title
is available from the British Library

Printed and bound in Great Britain
by Cox & Wyman Ltd, Reading, Berkshire

Contents

DILLY AND THE PIRATES

Not very long ago, I was sitting quietly in our garden reading when I heard screams inside the house.

Suddenly the back door flew open, and a small dinosaur shot out. It was Dixie, my little brother's best friend. Dilly himself followed, in hot pursuit.

'Land ho, and shiver me timbers!' shouted Dilly. He was waving a stick with some old rope tied to it. 'Your punishment be one thousand lashes, ooh aargh!'

1

As you might have guessed, Dilly had a new obsession. That's why he was wearing a hat with a skull and crossbones on it, an eye-patch, a stripy jersey, and my old wellington boots.

It started after a visit to our local library during the school holidays. They were having a Pirate Week. There were story-tellings, quizzes and events.

We went on the last afternoon, and the librarian said the week had been a great success. She thought practically every young dinosaur in the neighbourhood must have come.

Dilly was very impressed, and had been pretending to be a pirate ever since. Although, if you ask me, it was just an excuse for him to be even more badly behaved than usual.

'Please, Dorla!' begged Dixie. She dived behind my chair. 'Don't let him hurt me with that . . . that thing!'

'Silence, ye lily-livered landlubber!'
shouted Dilly. 'This be not a thing.
It be my cat-o'-nine-tails!'

'You'd better hope Mother doesn't
catch you, Dilly,' I said. 'You know she
doesn't like you playing rough.'

That morning Mother had warned
Dilly he would be in big trouble if he
wasn't nice to Dixie. The last three
friends who had come to play had left
crying.

'But I'm just being a pirate and it's *lots* of fun. You're enjoying yourself, aren't you, Dixie?'

'No,' sniffed Dixie, who was on the verge of tears.

'You aren't?' asked Dilly, his eyes wide with surprise. Then he shrugged. 'Oh well . . . *I* am,' he said. 'Avast, me hearty! Prepare to be flogged to within an inch of your life!'

I had to do something, of course. I couldn't just let Dilly hurt poor Dixie. Her ears had drooped, and she looked very scared. I can't stand to see anyone like that.

Besides, I was sitting between the two of them.

So I jumped up, grabbed the stick from Dilly's paw, and held it high above his head. He was absolutely furious, and kept yelling and leaping in the air to try and get it off me.

'What on earth is all this fuss about?' said a voice behind us. It was Mother. 'Calm down, Dilly. I should think the whole street can hear you making that awful noise.'

'It's Dorla's fault,' said Dilly quickly. He put on the expression Father calls his Swamp-Jelly-Wouldn't-Melt-In-My-Mouth look. 'She's been interfering in our game.'

'Don't listen to him, Mother,' I said. 'He's nothing but a fibber. I'll tell you what really happened . . :'

I explained everything. Mother was quite cross. She could see that Dixie was frightened.

'That's it, Dilly,' she said. 'I warned you. I think Dixie should go home. *You* can spend the rest of the afternoon in your room — and no TV!'

'That isn't fair!' squealed Dilly. 'I was only playing.'

'But you always go too far,' said
Mother. 'It's about time you realised
other dinosaurs have feelings, like you.

'What he needs is a taste of his own
medicine,' I said.

'Shut up, smelly belly,' snapped Dilly.
'I hate you.'

'That will do, Dilly,' said Mother,
firmly. 'From now on, you're going to
make an effort to be nicer to *everyone*,
and that includes Dorla.'

'But why should I be nice to *her*?' said Dilly. He stuck his tongue out at me. I did the same back to him.

'So that she'll be nice to you,' said Mother. 'Then maybe I'll get some peace and quiet. Anyway, you never know, there might come a day when you'll be glad you've got a big sister.'

Dilly stared at her as if she'd gone completely round the bend. For once I agreed with Dilly. But it turned out we were both wrong . . .

A week later, we heard some very exciting news. A Summer Fête was to be held at The Swamp to raise money for charity, and Mother said we were going. I couldn't wait.

Dilly couldn't either, mostly because he had found out he would be able to enter a fancy-dress competition. Guess what costume he chose to wear . . .

7

He already had his hat, eye-patch, stripy jersey and boots. Mother also painted some of his teeth black, and gave him some scars with make-up. She even made him a cardboard cutlass.

Dilly was sure he'd be the winner. But when we arrived, his face fell. The place was packed with families, and there were dozens of small dinosaurs — each one dressed as a pirate!

'It looks like Pirate Week at the library was even more successful than we thought,' said Father. 'Some of these outfits are amazing. Look at Dixie. Hers is terrific!'

Dixie came running over and asked if Dilly was allowed to play. She kept giggling, almost as if she had a secret she could barely hold in . . .

But I thought no more about it as she and Dilly scampered off. Mother and Father gave me some money, and said

I could look round on my own too, if I wanted. So we split up.

It was a great fête. I spent ages browsing. I bought a lovely tyrannosaurus-tooth bracelet, a book, some stationery, and a big stick of sugar-cane. I even had some money left over!

All the stalls had been set up in the entrance hall. No one was supposed to be wallowing. On the doors to the main part of The Swamp was a sign: 'No Entry'.

I was walking past them when I heard
something that stopped me in my tracks
It was the muffled, but still unmistakable
sound of Dilly's ultra-special, 150-mile-
per-hour super-scream.

I couldn't see Mother and Father in
the crowd, and I didn't know any of the
grown-ups nearby. So I decided I'd
better go in myself and find out what
my little brother was up to.

I pushed through the doors and
noticed several small dinosaurs near the

diving board. Another was actually teetering close to its end. It was Dilly, and he was pale green with fear.

I wasn't surprised that he was scared. Dilly can wallow, but he's not good enough yet to go out of his depth. And he knew the mud beneath the diving board was very, very deep.

'Land ho, and shiver me timbers!' one of the others shouted. It was Dixie, and she was prodding Dilly with his own cardboard cutlass. '*Your* punishment be to walk the plank, ooh aargh!'

Then I recognised the rest, and everything fell into place. Each of them had recently come to play with Dilly. Now they were taking their revenge!

I had to do something, of course. I couldn't just stand there and let Dilly be pushed into The Swamp. He was starting to blubber, and I can't stand to see anyone like that.

Besides, he is my little brother.

'OK, everybody,' I called out, trying to think of what Mother or Father would say in this sort of situation. 'Er . . . this game seems to have gone too far.'

'Dorla!' gasped Dilly. 'Boy! Am I glad to see you!'

For once, I'm sure he was telling the truth. I was helping him off the diving board when the grown-ups arrived . . .

Dixie's parents got her to admit she and the other three had planned the whole thing. But she claimed she would never have actually pushed Dilly in.

In any case, they were told off, said sorry, and made friends again. Later on, Dilly clapped and cheered along with everybody else when Dixie won the fancy-dress.

'Well, Dilly,' said Mother when we were leaving. 'I'm just grateful you're all right. But maybe you understand now what it feels like to have someone being horrible to you.'

'I do,' he said. 'And I won't be nasty to anyone ever again.'

'What, not even to Dorla?' said Mother, smiling.

'Especially not to my big sister,' said Dilly, looking up at me with big, soulful eyes. 'She's just wonderful.'

'Oh, yuk,' I said. 'Stop it, you're making me feel sick!' I was beginning to wish I hadn't saved him after all . . .

DILLY AND THE TV SHOW

'Shouldn't we have left by now, Mother?'
I said. I felt *so* excited. This was going to
be the most thrilling day of my life. 'The
TV company said that we mustn't be
late.'

'Stop worrying, Dorla,' said Mother,
stacking the last of the breakfast things
in the dishwasher. 'I'll just round up
your little brother, and then we can be
on our way.'

'But does Dilly really *have* to come?' I
said.

14

'Don't start all that again, Dorla, please,' sighed Mother. 'I've told you, it's not fair for Dilly to miss this. You wouldn't be appearing on TV in the first place if it wasn't for him. I wonder where he's got to . . .'

Mother headed out of the kitchen and went upstairs. She was right, of course, although it wasn't as simple as she made it sound. But then, nothing ever is where Dilly's concerned.

A few weeks back we visited the museum. Dilly misbehaved, as usual, and ran off. I found him with a camera crew from my favourite TV programme, *Swamp Mania*. They were doing an item on an exhibition about Marsh Moths, which are nearly extinct.

I'm very interested in endangered species. I think all dinosaurs should be, don't you? Anyway, because of something Dilly said, Donna, the

15

presenter, ended up inviting me to be on the show when they next covered conservation.

Someone from the *Swamp Mania* office called me on the dino-phone a few days later. I was given a date to come to the studio, and that date was . . . today!

'Are we all set?' said Father. He was standing in the hall with the keys to the dino-car in his paw.

'Almost,' said Mother, coming down the stairs. 'I was looking for Dilly. I sent him up to brush his teeth and get dressed ages ago. Have you seen him?'

Father said he hadn't, but just then we heard a noise. It seemed to be coming from the living room. Mother opened the door . . . and there was Dilly. He was sitting on the floor watching cartoons on TV, his snout very close to the set.

And he was still wearing his pyjamas.

I was horrified.

'But Mother,' I said. 'If he doesn't hurry up we'll be late!'

'Don't panic, Dorla,' said Mother. 'Dilly will now show us how fast he can get ready when he sets his mind to it — won't you, Dilly? Unless, that is, he doesn't mind being banned from watching a certain programme called *It's Amazing . . .*'

Dilly loves *It's Amazing*. It's on every week, and it's about breaking silly records, like who's got the longest tail in the world. I can't see the attraction. I think the only dinosaurs who watch it are those with the tiniest brains.

Anyway, Dilly's ears pricked up at Mother's words. A green blur shot out of the living room, up the stairs then down to the hall, where it turned back into a small dinosaur with shiny teeth and his dungarees buttoned up wrong.

'Come on,' he said. 'What are we waiting for?'

Mother and Father shook their heads, smiled, and gave each other that He's-Such-A-Horror-But-You-Do-Have-To-Laugh-At-Him-Sometimes look. I didn't think it was very funny. I was only interested in getting to the TV studio.

That proved more difficult than we had expected. There was a lot of traffic, and most of the time we just crawled along. After ten minutes without much progress I wanted to scream.

'This is your fault, Dilly,' I snarled. 'If we're late, I'll never speak to you again.'

'Great!' said Dilly. 'Could you drive more slowly, Father?'

'That will do, Dilly,' said Mother before I had a chance to blow my top.

Father sniggered, then pretended he was coughing. 'Relax, Dorla,' Mother continued. 'The traffic's clearing . . . Why don't you go through your folder?'

I did what Mother said, even though I'd learned everything in my Marsh Moths folder off by heart. I had worked very hard over the last week so that I would know exactly what to say when I was on *Swamp Mania*. I was completely prepared for it.

What I wasn't prepared for, though, was the size of the TV studios. We arrived at last, and were directed to a huge car park, then from there to an absolutely enormous building. Just looking at it made me feel nervous.

We went through some tall glass doors, and found ourselves in a very impressive room. Facing us was a long counter with a uniformed dinosaur sitting at it. The wall behind him was

filled with TV screens, each one showing
a different programme.

Another dinosaur bustled up to us.
He was tutting, and looked flustered
and harassed. His name was Dirk, and
he had been waiting for me. We weren't
late, but for some reason the
conservation item on *Swamp Mania* had
been brought forward. I had to go
straightaway.

'If you'd just follow me . . .' said Dirk. 'Your family can watch from here.'

'Excuse me,' said Dilly, suddenly, tugging at Dirk's sleeve. 'Isn't that *It's Amazing*?' He was pointing at one of the screens. Dirk said it was, they were recording a show that very morning. 'Oh, wow!' said Dilly, and began to bounce up and down with excitement. 'Can I go and watch? Please? Can I?'

'I'm sorry, but I don't think that would be possible,' said Dirk, snootily. He took my arm. 'If you don't mind . . .'

Dilly stopped bouncing immediately, and I had an awful feeling he was on the verge of making a scene. If he did, I didn't see it. Dirk hustled me into a lift. I heard Mother and Father call out 'good luck', but then they were gone.

I'd like to say I enjoyed what happened next, but the truth is . . . I didn't. Dirk rushed me to the *Swamp*

Mania studio, my feet barely touching the floor. Once we were there, I was shoved into a crowd of young dinosaurs surrounding Donna.

She was asking questions about conservation, and the others were shouting the answers. I was too dazzled by the powerful lights, and too confused by the cameras moving around to say anything. My mind went blank.

A few minutes later, it was over.

In the lift going back, I felt so disappointed I almost cried. Mother and Father said they'd seen me on one of the TV screens, but they couldn't cheer me up. I just wanted to go home.

'Er . . . there were *four* of you, weren't there?' said Dirk.

Mother and Father looked around, then at each other.

'Dilly!' they said together, in one strangled voice.

Oh no, I thought, that's all I need. Not only does my wonderful day at the TV studios turn out to be a flop, my pest of a little brother also decides to do his famous disappearing act. Mother, Father and Dirk ran off to find him.

I stood there feeling very sorry for myself. But then my eyes drifted to the wall of TV screens, where I saw something that made my mouth fall open with surprise. It was Dilly!

He had appeared on a screen at the top. He was at the back of the audience. Suddenly, he looked round, then scampered away. Seconds later, Mother, Father and Dirk were on the same screen. By now Dilly was three screens further along.

I realised what he was up to. He was searching through the building for the studio where *It's Amazing* was being recorded. He was soon lost, and kept popping up in other programmes, causing chaos and confusion wherever he went.

He made it eventually, and by the time he dashed out in front of the presenter for *It's Amazing*, the tears were dripping off my snout. But I wasn't unhappy. I was crying with laughter.

Dirk caught up with him, so Dilly let rip with an ultra-special, 150-mile-per-hour super-scream.

It didn't get him into trouble, though. In fact, the presenter thought Dilly was part of the show! 'What a noise!' he said once Dilly had finished. 'That must be a world record, folks. *It's amazing!*'

Then Dilly was interviewed in front of millions of dinosaurs. And do you know what he did? He insisted they bring Mother, Father and me into the studio to be on TV with him.

The dinosaurs on the *It's Amazing* team were very friendly. When the recording was finished, they showed us round their studio. They gave Dilly a book and me a T-shirt.

In the end my day did turn out to be exciting, thanks to Dilly. I have to admit I was glad he came with us, after all.

Just don't tell him I said so!

DILLY AND THE SURPRISE PARTY

'OK, Father,' said Dilly, who had a look on his face I've certainly seen before. 'You asked for it.'

Then he opened his mouth and . . . that's right, you guessed it, he let rip with an ultra-special, 150-mile-per-hour super-scream, the kind that shatters glasses full of pineapple juice and sends Father and me diving for cover until it's over.

You might think Dilly's scream shouldn't shock us any more, especially since we've been hearing it so often recently. This particular blast was the third he'd fired off that morning.

Believe me, you never get used to it.

'If you imagine a lot of noise is going to make me change my mind, Dilly,' said Father as we emerged from beneath the kitchen table, 'I'm afraid you're wrong. Only good little dinosaurs get taken to the park, and you've been very bad.'

'But what have I done, Father?' said Dilly innocently.

'What have you done?' squeaked Father. He looked up at the ceiling for a second, then back at Dilly. 'Give me strength . . .' he muttered under his breath. 'What haven't you done, rather,' he said. 'You've been appallingly behaved this week.'

'I didn't mean to break the window yesterday, Father,' said Dilly. 'It just sort of, er . . . got in the way.'

'Oh, did it?' said Father, folding his arms and tapping his foot. 'I suppose you didn't mean to kick a hole in the bathroom door during a tantrum, either? And that rude name you called Mrs Darma the other day, it just sort of slipped out, did it?'

'Well, I . . .' said Dilly.

'Spare me the excuses, Dilly,' said Father. 'You've been naughty, disobedient, bad-tempered . . .'

'*And* he's been horrible to me, too,' I

29

said. 'You mustn't forget that, Father.'

'Thank you, Dorla, I won't,' sighed Father. 'Not that I need to be reminded what with the pair of you fighting day and night. And I think most of the blame does lie with you, Dilly. You've been a little horror.'

'Have I really?' said Dilly with a big smile. He actually had the nerve to sound quite pleased with himself!

'Yes, you have,' said Father, in his sternest voice. Dilly's smile vanished. 'And I've just about had enough. Now go to your room and stay there. I don't want to see you until tea-time.'

Dilly tried to argue, but Father wasn't having any of it. So Dilly stomped off upstairs, STOMP, STOMP, STOMP. And even though we knew what to expect, Father and I both jumped when Dilly shut his bedroom door with a very loud . . . SLAM!

Mother arrived home from work a bit later.

'Hello, Dorla,' she said, and kissed me.

'Dilly's been naughty again,' I said.

'I think your mother had better hear it from me, Dorla,' said Father. 'Besides, don't you have some homework to do?'

I knew why he was trying to get rid of me. He wanted to talk to Mother about Dilly without yours truly around. Sometimes it's so easy to guess what your parents are up to, isn't it?

It's easy to fool them as well, or at least, that's what I thought. I started going slowly upstairs, and they went into the kitchen. But as soon as they couldn't see me, I shot down, tippy-toed over to the door, and eaves-dropped.

They had left it slightly open. I held my breath as Father told Mother about the latest Dilly disasters. He kept saying he couldn't understand why Dilly was being so awful. Then Mother said she thought she'd worked it out.

According to her, it was because of the surprise party they were organising for Grandma and Grandpa's 40th wedding anniversary. Dilly is always badly behaved when he isn't getting lots of attention, and they had been very busy.

'You're probably right, dear,' said Father. 'Perhaps we ought to try and spend more time with him. You don't think Dorla feels we've been neglecting her, too, do you?'

'Not really,' said Mother. 'Although we could ask her. I have the strangest feeling she's very near . . .'

Mother suddenly poked her head round the door and gave me her 'I-Know-What-You've-Been-Up-To' look. She made me jump, but I pretended that I had only just come downstairs again and was simply on my way to the living room. We both knew differently.

I didn't get told off though. Mother and Father were too worried about Dilly to give me a hard time.

If he kept being badly behaved, they said, he might ruin the party. He *has* nearly wrecked other family occasions in the past, after all.

So I wasn't surprised to see them being very nice to him during the next few days. It didn't have much effect, though. If anything, it seemed to make him worse. But then I could have told them that's what would happen.

I don't know why, but sometimes Dilly gets stuck in his bad behaviour mode, like a toy Dinobot with its wiring gone wrong. Something has to happen to help him get out of it.

Anyway, the big day arrived at last. It started off well enough. We had invited Grandma and Grandpa to our house for dinner. As far as they knew, it would be just us and them. What a surprise they got when they came through the door!

The whole family was there — all our aunts and uncles and cousins, as well as lots of friends. Everyone was standing under a banner some of the little

dinosaurs had made. It said: 'Happy
Anniversary To A Great Couple Of
Dinosaurs!'

We gave them three cheers, and
Grandma burst into tears.

She was soon smiling, though, just like
the rest of us. Mother made a short
speech, Grandma and Grandpa cut the
enormous cake Father had made, and
then the fun began. The only problem
was . . . Dilly.

It wasn't long before he started misbehaving. He didn't do anything spectacularly bad, but you could tell it was coming. So instead of Mother and Father enjoying themselves, they were following Dilly around with anxious looks on their faces.

After a while, Grandma asked me why they seemed so worried.

'Ah, I see,' she said when I'd finished explaining. 'I think this is a problem I can solve. Dilly,' she called out. 'Over here, please. I'd like a word with you.'

She was only just in time. Dilly was smirking wickedly as he quietly tugged at the table cloth under the cake. He quickly let go of it and came towards us.

'You're a big grown-up dinosaur, aren't you, Dilly?' said Grandma, and smiled at him.

'Yes, Grandma,' said Dilly proudly.

'Well then, I've got exactly the right

job for you,' said Grandma. 'Now, if you come along with me, I'll tell you what it is. We must find your Aunt Dimpla . . .'

Dilly looked as mystified as I felt, but we soon discovered what Grandma had in mind. She wanted Dilly to take care of our cousin Deevoo, Aunt Dimpla's oldest child.

Aunt Dimpla thought it was a terrific idea. She had her paws full with Didi, her new baby, and Deevoo was a very lively toddler these days. Recently, she said, he'd been a terror.

'In fact, I'm sure he's been feeling a little left out,' I overheard Grandma whispering to Dilly. 'So he might try to get some attention by being naughty, and that could spoil the party. We need someone to keep an eye on him . . .'

'Don't worry,' said Dilly, straightening his shoulders. 'You can rely on me . . .'

'That's what I thought,' said Grandma, giving me a wink.

Once Dilly had gone off with Deevoo, Grandma explained what she was doing. Giving Dilly some responsibility would make him less likely to be mischievous himself, she said. And Deevoo would probably keep him too busy to misbehave, anyway.

I had to admit it was a neat plan. But would it work?

Amazingly enough, it did. Dilly stuck to Deevoo like swamp moss to a giant fern. He seemed to know what Deevoo was going to do before he did it. I suppose that's because Dilly has done everything naughty it's possible to think of.

So in the end the party turned out to be a great success. Even Mother and Father were able to relax. But I was speechless when I heard what Dilly said the next morning.

'I'll bet you're really glad I'm grown-up now, and not like Deevoo any more, Father,' he said. 'You don't have to worry about me being naughty all the time, do you?'

'Well, I don't know about that . . .' said Father. But Dilly wasn't listening. He had already skipped away to play . . .

DILLY AND THE MIDNIGHT MONSTER

'Mother, have you seen Swampy?' said Dilly, skidding to a halt in the kitchen. 'I can't find him anywhere.'

'I do wish you wouldn't interrupt like that, Dilly,' replied Mother, crossly. 'Can't you see I'm talking to your sister? What was it you were saying, Dorla?'

'But, Mother,' said Dilly before I could carry on. 'This is important.'

'So is Dorla's news, Dilly,' sighed Mother. 'Anyway, Swampy will find you. He always does in the end.'

Swampy is Dilly's pet swamp lizard, and recently he's been a real nuisance. He keeps climbing out of his cage to look for Dilly, who panics when he sees the cage is empty.

'Good thinking, Mother,' said Dilly, and ran off.

'Now, where . . .' said Mother, wincing as Dilly shut the kitchen door with a BANG! ' . . . were we?'

I had been telling Mother about the trip I wanted to go on with my Greenie troop in a couple of weeks. My best friend Deena and I joined the Greenies last year, and we love absolutely everything about it — our uniforms, and working for badges, and singing songs and playing games. So you can imagine how thrilled we were when Mrs Deary, our troop leader, announced she had arranged a weekend expedition to Fern-Tree Hollow.

Mother said she thought it would be a lot of fun, and that I could go. We told Father about it that evening at dinner, and he made a brilliant suggestion.

'My old tent's in the loft,' he said. 'I'll help you put it up in the garden. You could invite Deena over tomorrow to spend the night with you in it.'

I was on the dino-phone to Deena almost before Father had finished speaking. Deena's mother said she could come.

The next day, Father found the tent and showed me what to do. It was much easier than I thought it would be. The only hard bit was banging the pegs into the ground, which was very dry because of the hot weather we've been having.

At least we had no interference from Dilly. His friend Darryl had asked him round to play, and he wasn't due back until later that afternoon. That gave us plenty of time to get everything ready for when Deena arrived.

Father had borrowed a couple of sleeping bags and a camping lamp, which we put inside the tent. I added some books, my radio, and plenty of sugar-cane for a night-time feast. There was only one thing missing — Deena.

At about five o'clock, the dino-phone rang. As soon as Father answered and

started speaking, my heart sank. Deena, it appeared, wasn't feeling well. She had a temperature, and was covered in spots. So she wouldn't be coming after all.

Which meant *I* wouldn't be spending the night in the tent, either. Father said he didn't think I should do it alone. I sat down on the grass feeling really fed up.

Just then, Mother brought Dilly home. Father explained to her what had happened. Dilly ran up to the tent and began asking questions about it. He didn't wait for any answers. He talked so fast there were no gaps between the words at all. And that's when I did something very strange.

'What if . . . Dilly took Deena's place?' I said.

The silence was so complete you could have heard a fern leaf fall. Mother, Father and Dilly were all looking at me

with their mouths open in surprise.

But I swear I hadn't gone crazy. It seemed like a good idea at the time. The tent was ready, and it would have been such a waste not to have used it. I didn't think Mother or Father would want to spend the night in it. That left Dilly.

He was so excited at the prospect his tail had curled up and was quivering. Mother and Father, however, were quite hard to persuade. They said they thought Dilly might be a bit too young, and that we were bound to argue.

'I promise we won't,' I said. 'You do too, don't you, Dilly?'

'Cross my heart and hope to die,' said Dilly, smiling . . . and they gave in.

A couple of hours later, Dilly and I brushed our teeth, changed into our pyjamas, and headed for the tent. It was a lovely, warm evening, and the sun was going down beyond the giant fern.

'Are you sure you'll be all right?' said Father. Dilly and I were in our sleeping bags. We both nodded. 'The back door isn't locked, and we'll keep an eye on you from the house . . .'

'Come on,' said Mother, pulling Father away. 'Stop fussing. They've got everything they need. They'll be fine. Night night, see you in the morning!'

We said night night back, and they

went indoors. I heard Father opening one of the upstairs windows. I zipped up the flap and lit the lamp. It was cosy.

I have to say it was also quite pleasant being with Dilly. I know I complain about him a lot, but he can be very nice when he wants to, and he was certainly making an effort on this occasion.

We listened to my radio for a while, then played I-Spy, which didn't take very long because there wasn't much in the tent. Then we ate the sugar-cane and told each other jokes. Dilly's were much ruder than mine, but very funny.

By now the sun had set, and it was pitch-dark in the garden. I was feeling rather tired, and said we ought to go to sleep. Dilly said OK, but only if I read him a story, like Father did every night.

'No problem,' I said. It made me feel good to be nice to my little brother. 'I've got just the right one, too. You like scary stories, don't you, Dilly?'

'Oh yes,' said Dilly eagerly. 'The scarier the better.'

I started reading from a book called *The Midnight Monster*. It's about a terrifying creature which roams the countryside at night. Some brave young dinosaurs kill it, but not before it's done some disgustingly gory things.

'Er . . . you can stop reading now, Dorla,' said Dilly eventually, in the middle of a very nasty passage.

'Oh, right,' I said, and switched off the lamp.

We said goodnight, and lay there quietly in the dark. Outside, the leaves on the giant fern rustled as the wind tossed them. I closed my eyes and tried to go to sleep, but all I could think of was monsters . . .

'Dorla,' whispered Dilly suddenly. 'Can you hear that?'

'What is it?' I whispered back.

'I don't know,' he said. 'A sort of scuffling noise near the flap. There it is again!'

I heard it myself that time.

'Don't worry,' I said. 'It's probably just something the wind's blown up against the tent. It will go away in a minute.'

But it didn't. The noise got louder. It began to sound as if something was trying to scrabble its way into the tent.

'I don't like it,' muttered Dilly, with fear in his voice. 'Do you think it's . . . *The Midnight Monster*?'

'Don't be silly, Dilly,' I said. 'It . . .'

Whatever was out there didn't give me a chance to say anything else. It jumped at the flap, making the whole tent shake. Dilly scrambled over to me and we sat hugging each other in fright. The thing kept leaping, and the tent kept shaking.

And finally, of course, Dilly fired off an ultra-special, 150-mile-per-hour super-scream, the kind that wakes up the *whole* neighbourhood and brings Mother and Father running.

It took them ages to calm us down. And I can tell you, we both felt pretty stupid when we discovered the terrifying, tent-attacking midnight monster was . . . Swampy!

He had got out of the house through

the window Father had left open, and come looking for Dilly. He was calmly sitting by the tent when Mother and Father arrived. We think Swampy actually likes Dilly's scream!

Dilly and I decided to spend the rest of the night indoors.

At breakfast the next morning, Dilly said he had only been so frightened because of the scary bedtime story I'd read to him.

'I was only trying to be nice,' I said.

'Maybe you'd better stick to arguing,' laughed Mother.

Somehow I don't think that's going to be very hard — do you?

Tony Bradman

DILLY'S MUDDY DAY

Dilly is the naughtiest dinosaur in the whole world. Especially when he doesn't get his own way.

Like the day he went to the park and rode his dino-trike into the swamp. And the time he wanted more pocket money and tried to open his own shop. But most of all you have to watch out for his ultra-special, 150-mile-per-hour super-scream!

Tony Bradman

DILLY GOES SWAMP WALLOWING

previously published as
Dilly the Worst Day Ever

In this fifth collection of stories about Dilly, the world's naughtiest dinosaur, dilly causes mayhem at the library, goes swamp wallowing and promises to be good for a whole year – but I don't think he can be, do you?

Tony Bradman

DILLY GOES ON HOLIDAY

Dilly and his family are off on holiday to the Swamp Land theme park. Dilly is sure he's going to have fun – but isn't too pleased when he finds that he's going to have to join the Tiny Tails. Then Dilly meets Dee who looks after the Tiny Tails – and decides that he's going to have a good holiday after all!

In this tenth book about Dilly the Dinosaur, Dilly also takes part in a Sports Day, puts on a magic show and finds a pet.

A Selected List of Fiction from Mammoth

☐	7497 1421 2	**Betsey Biggalow is Here!**	Malorie Blackman	£2.99
☐	7497 0366 0	**Dilly the Dinosaur**	Tony Bradman	£2.99
☐	7497 0137 4	**Flat Stanley**	Jeff Brown	£2.99
☐	7497 0568 X	**Dorrie and the Goblin**	Patricia Coombs	£2.50
☐	7497 0983 9	**The Real Tilly Beany**	Annie Dalton	£2.99
☐	7497 0592 2	**The Peacock Garden**	Anita Desai	£2.99
☐	7497 0054 8	**My Naughty Little Sister**	Dorothy Edwards	£2.99
☐	7497 0723 2	**The Little Prince (colour ed.)**	A. Saint-Exupery	£3.99
☐	7497 0305 9	**Bill's New Frock**	Anne Fine	£2.99
☐	7497 1530 8	**Who's a Clever Girl, Then?**	Rose Impey	£2.99
☐	7497 0041 6	**The Quiet Pirate**	Andrew Matthews	£2.99
☐	7497 0420 9	**I Don't Want To!**	Bel Mooney	£2.99
☐	7497 1496 4	**Miss Bianca in the Orient**	Margery Sharp	£2.99
☐	7497 0048 3	**Friends and Brothers**	Dick King Smith	£2.99
☐	7497 0795 X	**Owl Who Was Afraid of the Dark**	Jill Tomlinson	£2.99
☐	7497 0915 4	**Little Red Fox Stories**	Alison Uttley	£2.99